Incredible Snowman

Snowmen of Snowmass, Volume 1

PRESCILLA ROSS-YOUNG

Published by PRESCILLA ROSS-YOUNG, 2022.

Prescilla Ross-Young
www.PrescillaRoss-Young.one[1]
Image: www.postermywall.com

The Incredible Snowman

By
Prescilla Ross-Young
Copyright Prescilla Ross-Young 2012

---

1.   http://www.prescillaross-young.one

This is a work of fiction. Similarities to real people, places, or events are entirely coincidental.

INCREDIBLE SNOWMAN

First edition. March 2, 2022.

Copyright © 2022 PRESCILLA ROSS-YOUNG.

ISBN: 979-8201390129

Written by PRESCILLA ROSS-YOUNG.

Also by PRESCILLA ROSS-YOUNG

Here's Love
Here's Love, Once Again

Magic Doll
Her Magic Doll
His Mystery Doll

Snowmen of Snowmass
Incredible Snowman

?One?

Abigail Jackson was surrounded by her college friends. The expression on all their faces made her feel like she said the wrong thing. All she did was state that she would go to Snowmass Village and do what she did best, snoop.

"Come on, Abbey, what do you know about Colorado? Nothing, how are you going to get there? You have never seen snow in your thirty years of living." Jenny emphasizes with the wave of her hands.

"I'm the best private investigator you know. Hell, I'm the best PI in the whole state of Florida. You know me, I gather all the information I need to know about a place before I go. I will drive my Tahoe, it has all today's modern features, GPS system, satellite radio, seat warmers, heated side mirrors, and here's the kicker OnStar. I can stop by GMC before I leave and get some snow tires put on. We know that Marilyn needs this and I need to get away. I have no other jobs to do right now, so I'm free. I mean that money wise too."

"You know she's right Jenny. That's why we told her. I can afford to pay someone to do this but I know that Abbey will not stop until she gets all the answers." Marilyn stated trying to be the peacemaker. That was her, the forever peacemaker.

Abbey looked at her friends and still wonders how they all manage to continue to be strong friends. They were always there for each other. Like tonight, this gathering was actually for her. Todd, her ex-fiancé, was an outright asshole. Two days before their wedding he made a big hurtful announcement in the *Miami Tribute*. It still made her want to beat the stew out of him and her ex-business partner. She had to get away and this was her ticket out.

"I know that look, Abbey. It's the middle of October; can't you wait until spring to go?"

"I don't want to wait. You just told me that the lawyer who claimed that he helped with the adoption is dying. That means leave as soon as I can get my things packed."

"Come on, we all know she's right." Jaclynn said with no warmth. Her eyes were a piercing ice blue.

"Plus a change of scenery will do me good. I need to get away for a while."

Everyone nodded their heads slowly. Here they were a group of beautiful women with more than college in common: Abigail auburn hair with emerald green eyes, Valarie ebony hair with honey brown eyes, Marilyn chestnut hair with sapphire blue eyes, Jaclynn blonde hair and ice blue eyes, Tabitha with raven hair and silver grey eyes, Evelien with brunette hair with ocean green eyes and Katriel with burgundy and dark purple eyes. Of course Yasmina is always late.

"I promise I won't go up there and fall in love with the first man I see." Abbey stated with a smile. "I'm going to be focused. Plus I need to work on myself. I'll call you all when I stop to sleep and when I get there. I'm going to go pack."

"Just be careful, and when you get further up north, please buy a throw and a heavier coat. You will need it and don't give me that look." Tabby stated, with a knowing smile.

"Sorry that I'm late. What did I miss?"

"Not much Mina, let's see, Abbey's going to Colorado to see if she can find out why Marilyn was adopted."

"Wow, are you going flying or driving?"

"I'll be driving there. That way I'll have my own vehicle and be more comfortable. I'll stop in a couple of cities to get some rest. So I should be there in three or maybe four days. I promised to check in with all of you every night. Stop worrying, I'll be fine."

"What time are you leaving?"

"Well, I'm going to go home and pack now. That way I'll have all my things in the car before I leave. I will have to stop by the dealership before I leave to get some snow tires."

"Well, I'll come and help you pack." Yasmina stated. "I hope you got some warm clothes. I hear it's starting to get cold up there this time of year."

?Two?

Three days later, Abbey was wishing that she had listened to Tabby. She was in a big hurry to leave Miami. Not only she didn't get a heavier coat, they didn't even have snow tires. She had to order them and wait four days before they arrived. Not only didn't she have the time to wait, she didn't have the patience either. Her stop in Atlanta was short. It was just a place to lay her head. She had a time schedule to keep. It would be no good to her if she froze to death. Who would have thought that a blizzard would hit at this time of day and at this time of year? Now she was stuck in this ditch, in the middle of nowhere, eight miles from her destination with no help in sight. Apparently the OnStar was out of range, because no one answered when she pressed the button. It was a good thing that there was a blanket in her emergency kit that she brought with her.

Noland's day was almost over when he got a call from Becky. Her son told her that there was a black SUV in the ditch near their home. It being that he was the only person in the vicinity with a tow truck and a snow plow, he had to be the one to rescue the poor bastard. Why would anyone be out in this type of weather? Someone had to be just passing through, and not paying attention to the weather report. Well they are just going to have to get their car out of the ditch tomorrow. He'll give them a lift to town and come back to get it tomorrow. As he was approaching the mile marker that Becky told him the vehicle was near, he saw that it was almost completely covered in snow. Yep, this is going to cost the guy in the SUV plenty.

Abbey heard a vehicle approach but she was too tired to even raise her head. She prayed that it would be help that was on the way, but wasn't too stupid to put herself in any kind of trouble. There was a tap on her window. She raised her head slightly and what she saw made her faint dead away.

Noland never had that type of response before with rescuing someone. He had to do the worst thing in the world: he had to break her window to open her car door. It had started to sleet just a little, but he knew that the sleet would turn into a downpour. When she saw him knocking at the window he could tell that he scared her. She didn't scream, but he could see the fear in her eyes. It was smart of her to climb into the back seat to try to keep warm. It made it easier for him to be able to get her out the car without having to worry about getting a lot of glass off her. Carrying her to the tow truck was easy, opening the passenger door was the hard part. He had to do some hard maneuvering, but he managed. He also went ahead and towed her vehicle to his shop. Maybe towing it there would make up for his breaking and entering. He would have to repair her window and hope she would forgive him for the additional damage he caused.

?Three?

Abbey was trying to wake up. She couldn't get her eyes to open. She could hear two guys talking. The guy with a nice deep bass asked if she had frostbite.

"No, Noland you got to her in the nick of time. She's going to be fine after a few hours of sleep."

"She's been sleeping since I found her."

"You needn't worry. Her body is tired; she put it through a lot by being out there in the cold. I advise you to go take a shower and get some sleep yourself. She'll be up in the morning asking you questions."

All Noland could do was nod his head. He had questions of his own. Why was she not listening to the weather channel, where was she going, and why did she have to come now in the middle of a blizzard? He has seen some beautiful women before but this one took the cake.

After letting the doctor out, Noland went back into his guest room to look at his unexpected guest. All he could do was look at her and wonder. He has never been a sucker for red hair, but hers was like a red and brown mixture, that he has never seen on someone before. He knew for a fact that it was her true hair color and not bottled by the other hairs that he saw on her body. Her body was solid and felt wonderful. Her skin wasn't milky white, which most redheads are known for. It had more of a coffee with a lot of cream in it color. Maybe she did a lot of tanning. He couldn't wait to see her in a nice fitting dress or a nice bathing suit. So he could see those curves he felt and caught a glimpse of when he had to get her out of her damp clothes. The only reason why she had damp clothes was because the weather had started sleeting. Then by the time he got her to his house the sleet turned into an outright downpour of rain, which made his driveway full of slush. He pulled his vehicle into the garage, which he was glad he kept now, because after changing vehicles at the shop he wasn't sure if his unwanted guest wouldn't catch a cold after all. He did enjoy carrying her around of course, it gave him a chance to feel her weight on him and he could get a handful of her curves. He thought about putting her in a tub of warm water but that would have been pushing his luck. He had to keep thinking of taking apart a motor to keep from thinking about her curves while he was toweling her dry to get her warm. He was really glad when the doctor rang the doorbell. He needed the distraction. Now it was just him and her in his home and he really could use a distraction now.

He could just picture her spreading her legs... okay maybe he did need to take that shower the doctor suggested and go to sleep. But it's going to have to be a cold one.

?Four?

When Abbey finally opened her eyes, the sun was bright and shining. All she could remember was that there was a dark monster that was knocking at the window. Then she tried to wake up because two guys were discussing her. She had no idea where she was and how she got there. Looking around she saw that someone had brought some of her bags, also. There was a knock at the door, and then it opened. All she could do was stare at the most handsome man she had ever seen in her life.

"I'm sorry did I startle you? It seems like I've been doing that a lot lately."

Not only was he handsome he had that nice soothing deep voice she heard earlier.

"What do you mean lately?" She asked after clearing her throat.

"Last night, I knocked on your car window to see if there was anyone in it and you fainted."

"That was you? You scared me half to death. I thought you were a Sasquatch or a Yeti."

"Well, I'm not bigfoot or the abominable snowman. I'm Noland Snow."

"Abigail Jackson. How did you just happen to be on that road last night?"

"I got a call last night that there was a SUV stuck in the ditch." At her confused look he explained. "I'm an auto mechanic and the only one near here with a tow truck and a snow plow."

"Where is here?"

"You are on the outskirts of Snowmass Village."

"You own Snowmass Village?"

"Well my ancestors built the ranch and some of the family still lives there."

"Oh."

"Just oh. Where were you headed, Ms. Miami?"

"To Snowmass Village, if you must know."

Noland thought to himself, oh hell here's another female, on that get rich skim. She was pretty too, but he knew the game. How many females have his brothers and he seen, wanting to snag one of the rich bachelors? He didn't know that their bachelorhood had reached all the way down to Florida.

"Well your SUV is in the shop. It needs some repairs done to it and you need some more days of rest."

"Repairs, what kind of repairs are you talking about?"

"Your front end has a few minor damages and your window. Don't worry I'll pay for the damage to the window."

"You broke my window?"

"How else was I going to get you out of the vehicle? Your doors were locked and you passed out while you were in the backseat. So I did the best thing I could think of. I made sure that I removed the few pieces of glass away from you gently so you would not get any cuts on you."

"Wow, I've met myself, a true hero."

Her sarcastic tone did not go unnoticed with him. His eyes flared with a warning.

"Here, eat your soup and I'll be back."

Their hands brushed each other and there was an electric shock that ran up both of their arms. Abbey looked at Noland with sexy shocked eyes and he couldn't resist the wanting he saw.

"I was hoping that this could be avoided."

"What?"

Before Abbey could grasp his meaning, Noland was caressing her lips with his. At her slight moan, Noland slipped his tongue between her parted lips.

"If you don't let go of her, she will be wearing the soup instead of eating it."

"Hi, Mom, you have perfect timing as always."

?Five?

"Mom, this is Abigail Jackson. I pulled her car out of a ditch last night. Her best bet was not to be dropped off at a hotel since she was not awake. Abigail, this is my mom."

"Hello, Mrs. Snow. You can just call me Abbey."

"So, Abbey, what brings you up here?"

"I'm looking into some things for a friend of mine. Where's my phone, where's my purse?"

"I left your purse downstairs on the table. I'll be right back."

"My son called me to come and look after you, but you don't look like you need any looking after."

"Mrs. Snow, I want to apologize for kissing your son."

"Are you sorry that it happened or sorry you got caught?"

"Sorry that we got caught." Abbey responded confused. Why did she give that answer?

"I've been where you are several times. I have eight sons and they all took after their father in looks and height. So I know the effect the Snow men have on women."

"It can't look good on my part, Mrs. Snow."

"Call me, Linda. I've never seen my son act so." Hearing her son's approach she stopped talking.

"Don't stop on my account. Never seen me act like what mom?" Walking past his mom to hand Abbey her purse.

"What I was thinking is not important. So you want me to babysit a grown woman?"

"Dr. Hall said that Abigail needs someone to keep a close watch on her. I can't do that if I'm at the shop all day."

"Why do I need someone to keep a close watch on me?"

"It's just a precaution that he's taking to make sure you don't get the flu or a head cold. You were out there in the cold and I don't know for how long. Plus it rained pretty darn hard last night so you got soaked with me having to carry you from one vehicle to the next. He was glad to see that you didn't have frostbite."

"Why am I the only one who got soaked?"

"That would be simply because I had on a raincoat. It would make no sense for both of us to get wet."

"I guess you're right on that one. How long am I going to be stuck here?"

"At least a week until Dr. Hall gets back."

"Where did he go?"

"On vacation, he left early this morning."

"I can't be stuck in this house for a week. I have things that I must do and people that I must see. Lying in this bed is not going to help me get them done."

"Hi, don't shoot the messenger. I didn't make you drive in that blizzard. I have to go to work, I'll see you later. If there's anything you need, don't be afraid to ask."

?Six?

"He didn't say that you had to stay in bed for the whole week. That you just must stay here. Here as in this town. Eat your soup and call your friends to let them know you are safe. I'll be downstairs, just holler when you're finished and I'll show you around the house."

Sitting her soup on the nightstand, Abbey opened her purse to look for her cell phone. Praying that she had some bars in this town, she turned it on. She never drove anywhere with her cell phone turned on. She read too many headlines about car accidents that were caused by people on their phones. She had a bar but could tell that her signal wasn't strong. Getting out of the bed, she realized that she only had on a robe.

Damn that man. I know he's the one who got me out of my clothes. At least she had a robe on. It could be worse because she could be naked. He did say that she was soaked last night and she knew for a fact that his mom was not over last night. Not knowing whether to be upset or not, Abbey went ahead and looked for her purple laptop bag. To say she had a thing for purple was an understatement. All her luggage bags were purple. As soon as Dell made a purple laptop she bought it, not caring that the one she had only had a few months use on it. She had to have purple everything. She tried dyeing her hair purple and purple contacts, they just didn't look right on her.

Grabbing her laptop bag, she took out her laptop. She hoped Noland had some type of internet service. She saw that he did, it didn't require a password, and logged on. She had a lot of email messages from Marilyn. She knew that Marilyn would be more upset than anyone else. Her lack of calling last night really caused Marilyn to go into an email message frenzy. Everyone started with 'why haven't you called'. Now the last one was a shocker. It actually had the word hell in it. With a smile Abbey replied to Marilyn messages and let her know she was okay. Also in her message was to contact her on her cell phone and not at the hotel. She left the lame excuse that she would never be in the room, so Marilyn wouldn't have a reason to call there.

She was afraid to include the part where she was driving in the middle of a blizzard. She'll tell her that one later. Marilyn would blame herself for Abbey's accident. Abbey didn't want to have her flying up here for no reason. And she really couldn't let her know she kissed a guy after only knowing him a few hours, well really minutes. How was she going to explain to Marilyn that she didn't quite make it to the hotel, without telling her about driving into a ditch? She would have to think of something or maybe not since Noland said that he was repairing her vehicle. I hope I don't regret not telling Marilyn that I didn't make it to the hotel, she thought as an afterthought.

?Seven?

Noland was very distracted at work. His secretary, Lily, could tell that something was on his mind. She had to repeat everything to him twice before she got his attention. Lily has never seen her boss like this. The only reason she took this job was to get his attention. All the Snow men were very handsome, but to her Noland took the cake. He never paid her much attention at all. She has always had a huge crush on him.

"Noland, what's her name?"

"Who's name?"

"I've worked with you for five years and I have never seen you the least bit interested in anything that has nothing to do with this shop. So what is her name?"

"I do not know what you're talking about."

"Really, then tell me why you have filled out the same invoice three times? Are you trying to charge Dr. Walker three times for the same job?"

Noland knew that Lily was right. He was very distracted by his unwanted houseguest, but wasn't about to tell her that. He knew that Lily had a crush on one of his brothers, but she has been able to remain professional. He knew that he shouldn't have kissed her. Her mouth looked so sweet and lushed, that he couldn't resist. Abigail's body was so curvy, it called for attention. That was how a woman should be built. Glancing up he noticed that Lily was still waiting on an answer.

"I don't know why I filled it out three times. I guess I should have gone to bed on time last night. My brain is still asleep right now."

"Do you need to go home early?" Lily asked with concern.

"No, because I still won't go to sleep. I'll find something to do at home. When did Glasco say they would have the window delivered?"

"It can't be here any earlier than Friday. They didn't have it in stock and had to order it. Do you want me to see if they can rush it?" Lily asked as an afterthought, when she saw his factual expression.

"No, that's okay. I'll have to inform Ms. Jackson that her vehicle is going to be ready later than expected."

"Who's Ms. Jackson? Do I know her at all?"

"No, she's someone who's just passing through, and she had a little car trouble. It's nothing to worry about."

"Are you trying to reassure me or yourself?"

Noland didn't say anything because he wasn't sure how to answer the question. If he said her, then she would think that he was interested in her. If he said himself then she would know that he was interested in Abigail. Funny, Abbey told his mom that she could call her Abbey, but not him. That's okay, he liked Abigail anyway.

?Eight?

"Abbey, are you okay in there?"

"Yes, Ms. Linda. I'm trying to find some clothes to put on. Everything that I have is for warmer weather."

"Would you like for me to go to the house, I can bring you back some sweaters?"

Abbey opened the door, and nodded.

"It wouldn't be a bother would it, if so I could probably borrow a shirt of Noland's."

"No it would be any trouble at all. I'm glad that you have some jeans. Where are you from?"

"Miami, Florida. I had a friend of mine advise me that I would need warmer clothes. I was in a hurry to get away. I figured I would have time to shop, once I got here."

"Don't put off what you need to do today for tomorrow, because tomorrow never comes. Plus having a blizzard and rain storm in the middle of October is unusual."

"Yep, that's something my mom always said to me. I try not to put off but, I really needed to get away. Florida is the wrong place to try to buy some winter clothes."

"So that means you don't have any long johns. What size do you wear?"

"A large should do, if they run smaller than most clothes then I'm going to need an extra large."

"Okay, come with me so I can show you around the house. From what I understand you were unable to see any part of the house last night."

Abbey slowly came out of the room. She wasn't sure how Linda would respond to her size. She wasn't a small girl and she knew it. She had more curves on her than any of her high school associates. She couldn't call them friends. Of course, her mom told her not to worry about her size, because there will be a man out there who will love her curves. Abbey thought she had found that guy in Todd, but he turned out to be a skinny woman type of guy.

"I'm glad to see you are not one of those women who believe in having only water and a lemon. Those skinny girls drive me crazy. I have yet to see why television always shows these thin behind women. All the women I've run into in my life are not a size zero or two. Now, I see why my son reacted to you, like he did. He wants a real woman with meat on her bones."

Laughing at what Linda said Abbey only took her words at face value. She figured that Linda was only trying to make her comfortable about her size.

"I got plenty of meat to give to someone else."

"No, you are not fat. I can see that you are very well toned. I know a lot of women who would kill to have the curves you have. Come on, I'll show you where everything is downstairs, then I'll go get you some sweaters or at least long sleeve shirts."

?Nine?

Getting a tour of the house was just what Abbey needed. She was shown the other bedrooms upstairs. She made note to ask Noland about their connecting rooms. The living room downstairs was phenomenal. It could have been a showroom, but it wasn't. It had that live-in feeling. When she was shown the kitchen, she almost fainted. It was her dream kitchen right here in his house. It was like he had been in her brain and could see what would make her the happiest. Double oven glass top stove, wrap around counter space, a huge island in the middle of the kitchen. This man knew a way to a man's heart was through his stomach and a way to get there was a great kitchen.

"Noland's favorite part of the house is the kitchen."

"I can see why, this is my dream kitchen we are standing in. Wow, it looks better in person than in the pictures."

"This kitchen is well used, so I don't think Noland would mind if you cooked something."

"Oh, man I can't wait."

"He keeps everything well stocked, refrigerator, cabinets and his freezer chest."

"I didn't see a freezer chest. Did I overlook it?"

"I'll show you where it's located."

Linda opened a small panel door that was well hidden.

"Noland got the idea off of *Misery*. He loves that movie. It was a fallout shelter, some time ago. He got rid of the other entrance."

The walkway was wide enough for only one person to walk down or up at a time. The light switch was at the entrance of the door. There was another light switch at the foot of the stairs. Abbey could see several doors, with names on each door, Entertainment, Errand, Relaxation, Tranquility and Provisions.

"I know that some of the names are common sense. The errand room is where you will find the washer, dryer, iron and iron board.

Relaxation room is where a pool, spa, and a sauna is located. I have yet to understand why his exercise room is called tranquility, that's not peace. In the entertainment room you have whatever you like to play as for games in that room. Provision room is where you can find the freezer and extra supplies pertaining to food. There are two bathrooms down here, one for males and other for females."

"This is a big house, for just one person to live in."

"That's what I told him, but he got a good deal on the house. Plus, he wants a big family with lots of get-togethers, or at least that's what he told me. It does have a big yard. Well let me go get you some sweaters."

?Ten?

Alone, Abbey went upstairs and looked around in Noland's room, until she found an old college sweater of his to put on. After that she went into the room she had been using and retrieved her forgotten soup. Her luck had to change soon. Not that she wasn't grateful that Noland had saved her, but she had to remember that her main reason for being here. Finding her friend's parents should be easy and would be easier if she didn't have him as a distraction. Noland was a big distraction, she wasn't close to falling in love, but she did like what she has seen so far.

Abbey had no idea what time Noland normally came home, but she figured that he would be hungry when he came home. The best way to show her appreciation to him was to cook dinner. Maybe, while he was eating she could convince him that their arrangement would not work.

After washing out her dish, she went down to his Provision's room to see what he kept in stock. All she saw in his freezer was beef, ground, steaks, and ribs. She could grill some hamburgers for him with no problem.

Now all she needed was to see what type of sauces he carried. She looked in his fridge to find two big juicy steaks. Man, the things she could do to steaks. She put the ground beef in the fridge and grabbed the steaks. She looked around until she found everything she would need to prepare the meal she had for him in mind. She would slow cook the steaks in the oven with some grill seasoning. She just hoped he liked spicy foods. Dang she wished she had the phone number to where he worked so she could call him. That way she could find out what he liked, what time he would be home and if it was okay for her to be taking over his home the way she did? She tried to cook over at Todd's house one time as a surprise and he flipped out on her. His words were never, mess with a man's domain without his permission. Of course, he would always complain about her cooking anyway. He did not eat this or that's not the way my mom cooked it. She had to be honest though it didn't look like Noland had any problem with eating. He had his place well stocked with food. Todd would only have a few items in his fridge and would always eat out. His kitchen had the bare minimal stuff in it. Noland kitchen was what one would call a kitchen. Maybe she should make a batch of cookies with the steaks. Nope that would be a little over the top. She wants to thank him, not give the impression she's trying to butter him up. Plus he might not even like her cooking. Okay only positive thoughts for now on.

?Eleven?

Pacing back and forth in his office, Noland was driving himself crazy. All he could do was think about Abbey. He wanted to rush back home just to make sure he didn't dream her up. She was perfect, in every aspect of the word. The perfect height, weight, size and feel about her. He couldn't believe that he kissed her. Hell, if his mom hadn't come into the room when she did, he would have pushed Abbey down on the bed. A lot more than kissing would have been going on. It's a fact, which can be proven by the way she was responding to his kisses. Why did he have to kiss her? True kissing wasn't a sin, but it does lead to other types of sins. Maybe he should call the house and see what his mom and Abigail were doing. No, that was childish. What made her so different from all the other females that he knows?

Noland was not what one would call an impulsive man. So, closing the shop early really shocked Lily and him. It wasn't the fact that he couldn't wait to see Abigail. It was the fact that his mom was right. It didn't make sense that she should have to babysit a grown woman, especially one that was stuck at his house. He knew she couldn't go anywhere because he had her SUV, but that didn't stop him from worrying that she would try to leave anyway. He was looking forward to going home. Now that he thinks about it, closing early did have a lot to do with Abigail. He couldn't wait to interact with her at the dinner table or in the living room. He should have stopped and ordered some take out at China City. Oh well, he could cook those steaks he put in the fridge. He would convince her to sit at the island and watch him cook. That way he could ask her questions and watch her at the same time. He wanted to see how she looked inside his house, how at ease she was among his things. What he couldn't understand was why he acted like this was his first date with his school crush? It was a good thing his brothers could not see him now. They would terrorize him so bad. Hopefully, by Sunday he will have his reactions under control. Pulling into the yard, he didn't bother with the garage, because he would be leaving again, once he found out what she liked to eat. Cooking would take too long and he wanted to.

The aromas that were coming out of the house stopped his thought and him in his tracks. He didn't think he was starving, but his stomach started growling. Looking back, he had to ensure himself that he didn't overlook his mom's car. Noland was quickly unlocking the kitchen door, because he was afraid that his mom might have left the food unattended. The sight he saw when he opened the door would forever be implanted into his brain.

?Twelve?

Abigail was excited about her grilled jalapeno steaks that were cooking in the oven. She just hoped Noland liked spicy foods. Bending over to check the steaks in the stove, she missed Noland's reflection in the mirror. Noland watched her until she stood back up. He walked quickly up on her, causing her to jump.

"Noland, you scared me. I wasn't sure what time you normally came home. Your mom showed me around the house, I hope you don't mind. Why are you staring at me like that?"

"I've never had a woman cook for me before, other than my mom. It's nice and scary at the same time."

"It's just a thank you dinner. Don't read too much into it."

"Why do you keep walking away from me and circling the island?"

"You make me very nervous. I really don't like the look you have in your eyes."

"What kind of look do I have?"

"Like you haven't eaten for days and I'm your last meal and you are a starving man."

"I promise you that I won't hurt you." He stated before pulling her toward him and seizing her mouth.

She tasted the same as this morning. Like a summer's day kissed with a little rain shower, fresh. He picked her up and placed her on the island. He straddled her legs and placed his hands under the shirt she had on. Her chest was aching to be touched and he knew all the right spots and ways to touch it. It was like he could read her mind. Light bites on her neck, tiny circles on her nipples with his thumb. Noland pulled her closer so she could feel how much he wanted her. His answer was a loud noise crossed between a moan and a surprised cry. Abbey started pulling his shirt out of his pants. She wanted to feel his chest to see if it was as hard as it felt.

"Noland, why is it every time, I come into your house you are harassing her? Do I have to take her home with me?"

Burying her face into Noland's neck, Abbey realized that she once again let her feelings overrule her conscience.

"Noland, you got to move, so I can get the shirts from your mom." Abbey whispered.

"If I moved right now, I would show mom how bad I really want you."

"Okay. Linda, I'll meet you upstairs as soon as I tell Noland what to do with the steaks."

"When I come back down, Noland, you and I are going to have a little talk."

"Damn, that's twice in one day, what are the odds?"

"Seems pretty high in your case, now move."

"Look, I'm sorry."

"For what, getting caught or starting something you can't finish?"

"Oh, I can finish alright." He stated while pushing her up against the island.

"I don't think so. I didn't come up here to get entangled with anyone. I won't lie to you or myself, yes I am attracted to you, but I have a job to do and a life to get back to. Plus, I don't sleep with everyone I'm attracted to."

Noland watched Abigail walk out of his kitchen, and made a promise to them both. That there will be some entangling before this was all over, but for right now he had to deal with two things. One was getting his erection to go down quickly. The other would be far easier, his mom. He loved her dearly, because he already knew what she was going to say. So all he had to do was beat her to the punch. Thinking about the sermon she was going to give him got rid of his first problem.

"Noland, I'm shocked at you."

"Mom, I doubt you are more shocked than I am at myself."

For the first time in his life his mom had no comeback.

"I don't understand, is it because she's different or because she's someone new?"

"I really can't say, son."

"Every time I get near her, I have this strong desire to kiss her. I don't even know her."

"Well, it seems like your body does."

"I don't believe in reincarnation. I can't build a relationship on lust. She's here on a job assignment then she's going back to Miami."

"Noland, bring her to dinner on Sunday anyway. You can't just leave her at the house by herself. She has no friends up here."

"What mom, no comment on my wanting a relationship with her?"

"That's because at this moment I know your relationship is a sex relationship. Plus it's no telling how long she'll be here. So that might change and she might stay."

"Of course she could run for the hills after Sunday, too."

"Noland she's..."

"What is it mom?"

"I love you."

"I love you too, mom. What were you going to say?"

"Never mind, it's not important right now."

Abbey was coming down as Linda was leaving out.

"Goodbye, Abbey"

"Goodbye, Linda. Will I see you tomorrow?"

"Yes, I'll come by after Noland has left for work." Thinking that would be a safe time to come since every time he's near her, he's kissing her.

"Okay. Thank you for the sweaters."

Walking by Noland, Abbey went into the kitchen to get the steaks out of the stove. The steaks had been in there long enough to be cooked just right for her taste.

Noland decided that he would be wise if he set the table while Abbey was in the kitchen. He would have to give her a key to his house at some time but hasn't been able to find the right time to approach the subject of her needing a house key.

?Thirteen?

After Noland set the table, he went into the kitchen to see if Abigail needed any help.

"What can I do to help?"

"Tell me what kind of vegetables you would like to get with your steak?"

"I like all kinds of vegetables. So you can just pick one and I eat it. Would you like for me to make us a salad?"

"That would be nice. I was thinking that maybe some broccoli and cheese casserole. I know that I'm cooking in your kitchen without permission."

"Hmm, that sounds good, and to think I was going to ask you what kind of takeout you would like."

"We can have take-out another day. I hope it's okay; I called the hotel I was supposed to be staying at." Seeing him nod his head, she kept going. "I cancelled my reservation. Since I don't have any form of transportation right now and I am stuck at your house."

"Wow, you just made it all sound better with that statement. Your SUV won't be ready until Friday. The window won't get here until then."

"I didn't mean to sound ungrateful. It's just that I have other plans and being unable to get around isn't helping."

"I take it mom didn't show everything."

"Everything, what do you mean?"

"Come."

Following Noland, he leads her to the other door off the kitchen.

"See here, other forms of transportation. The keys are located right on that hook behind you. Just two things, make sure you lock up the house and drive carefully. I have a spare key to give you to the house. Since you brought it up I feel better about saying that you need a key."

Too excited to say anything, she threw her arms around his neck.

"Okay, you have to get down before you start something."

"I'm sorry. How can I ever pay you back?"

"You can repay me by going to Sunday dinner with me. Mom has invited you. It's where all of us, her children, come home so she can fuss over us."

"Okay. You can count me in."

"I must warn you, you and mom might be the only females there."

?Fourteen?

After four days of coexisting and no more mishaps, Abbey felt good. She got to talk to a few of the doctors and nurses that were around some years back. She just couldn't get to the adoption lawyer. He was an extremely busy man. That was okay, she can talk to him on Monday. Today was Friday, and Noland would be here any minute to pick her up to get her SUV. She couldn't wait. It's nothing like having your own. Not that, Noland's car wasn't great, it was. It just wasn't her baby.

Smiling from ear to ear when Noland came in, Abbey didn't pay attention to his hesitation. When she was at the door and he wasn't behind her, she stopped.

"What's wrong, Noland?"

"Wow, I've never seen you smile before. You should do it often. You are very beautiful."

Her smiling took some of Noland's heart and he knew it. Now he's going to have to do a lot to keep her smiling.

Looking serious, Abbey just nodded.

"Look, I didn't mean to make you stop smiling. I was just being honest."

"I know. It's just that I've heard that line so many times it gets old."

"Believe me Abigail I wasn't feeding you no line."

"Really, that's good to know."

"So why are you so happy?"

"To have my car back is a wonderful thing."

Walking to the car, she was trying to figure out why Noland was walking beside her. Then he shocked her by opening her door. No man had ever opened her door for her. She was already a quarter way in love with him and he was trying to take all of her heart. Leaning over, Abbey opened his door. She was always taught to return the favor.

They arrived at his shop in fifteen minutes. It was in town, but not on the main street. That's how she never saw it while in town.

"Abbey, I was taught that a man always opens a ladies door."

"I'm sorry. I'm not used to men opening my door. To be honest you are the first. So let's make a deal. You open it for me to get in and I'll open it to get out."

"Now you are going to have to explain that to my parents."

With a big grin on her face, she nodded.

"Noland, while you were out your dad called to make sure that you were going to bring Abbey on Sunday." Lily stated while sending daggers at Abbey.

"Okay. Abigail this is Lily, Lily Abigail. I'll go get the keys to your SUV."

"So, you are the reason why Noland is all distracted. I don't see what he sees in you. Yeah, you got a pretty face but you are way too fat and too tanned for him. No man wants a fat woman, who can roll over and squash him."

"Here are your keys, Abigail. Abigail, what's wrong?"

"Nothing's wrong, Noland. Thank you. I'll see you later."

"Abigail?"

"Oh, how much do I owe you?"

"Nothing, I've already covered it."

Abbey couldn't wait to get out of his shop. She hated being called fat and she hated ones who assumed more. Plus her skin color was natural. She got her vehicle now; nothing was stopping her from checking into a hotel. She could always go to the doctor's office on Monday.

?Fifteen?

Abbey was almost finished packing up her SUV, when Noland arrived.

She didn't know Noland came home early to take her out. She was on the phone with her mom with her back to the room door.

"Mom, I'm telling you I had to hold my tongue. She pissed me off so bad. Where does she get the nerve to call me fat? She wished she had my body so she could turn a few heads."

"Who is she, so I can let her know that you are not fat?"

Looking shocked, Abbey couldn't say anything for a minute.

"Mom, I need to let you go. I have to handle something right now. I'll call you back a little later. I love you too."

"Noland, how long have you been there?"

"Long enough to know that; one you were talking to your mom, two someone called you fat, three you had to hold your tongue and four that you are packing." Noland was blocking the door and his arms were crossed. Abbey didn't know him well enough to know that was his don't try to lie to me stance.

"It's not what it seems?"

"Maybe you need to explain it to me, because it seems like you are leaving because someone I know called you fat."

"Okay, it might be what it seems a little bit. Don't get mad. You don't need me messing up your life."

"If you were messing up my life, so to speak, don't you think I would have told you?"

"Not if you are being nice."

"Nice, I don't do this when I'm being nice. Now one more time, who called you fat?"

"She doesn't matter."

"If she didn't matter, you would not be leaving, and leaving without telling me."

"She honestly doesn't matter. Noland, believe me, she doesn't matter. I don't want you to be angry with anybody."

"Now who's being nice, you don't owe her anything. So why are you doing it?"

"I'm the outsider in this town, not her. I know that this is a nice little community where everybody knows everybody. Just let it rest okay."

"On two conditions, you stay here; I'll help you unpack your vehicle and you go out with me tonight. Both conditions must be accepted together, no and ifs or buts about it."

"Noland, I don't understand why you are being so difficult?"

"I'm not trying to be difficult at all. I was very happy when I pulled up, until I saw your car with almost all your stuff in it. I was a little pissed. Then to overhear part of your conversation, with your mom, that really pissed me off more a closer notch toward the highest degree. I want you to be honest with me all the time and I will do the same in return."

"Noland, what I don't understand is why? You can have any female you want, why waste your time with me?"

"I don't see it as wasting my time. Now do you accept my conditions or are you going to give me her name?"

"Okay, I'll accept your conditions only if you will truly leave it alone."

"I will truly leave it alone unless I hear of someone else calling you fat." He kissed her to silence anything else she might have said. She could feel the pinned up anger in him when he kissed her.

?Sixteen?

Abbey was glad she agreed to go out with Noland. It was exactly what she needed. She hadn't realized how much she missed dinner clubs until they went out. She really wasn't a club person, but dancing and eating always interested her.

"Abbey, what do you do as a profession?"

"I'm a private investigator."

"Your assignment is all the way up here?"

"I'm tracking down someone's history for them. I really can't talk about it."

"No, I understand it's cool. What made you want to be a private eye?

"I like working on my own assignments on my own terms. You can't do that working for the government or for someone else. I studied law and business law in college."

"Plus you get to name your own price. That's got to be nice."

"What about you? Did you know you wanted to be an auto mechanic?"

"Yes, I was young and working on everything that had a motor. I couldn't see myself as a farmer. Good thing my parents had a lot of children."

"Your mom told me that there are eight of you. There are three of us, and I happened to be the only girl. Life was hard for me, an older and a younger brother. My dad was already enough, but my brothers made my life hell. I couldn't wait to get out of the house and go to college."

"See, we both have something in common."

"What do we have in common?"

"We are both second born and couldn't wait to get out of the house."

"You are so silly, but that is true."

"Care to dance?"

"I thought you would never ask."

As soon as they got on the dance floor, Noland knew he was in trouble. Abbey had very sexy and snake-like moves. It wasn't that he couldn't keep up, it was trying not to get too aroused.

The dress she had on was a fitting low cut black dress. He knew he was in a little trouble but now he was well over his head.

?Seventeen?

On the trip home, Noland was very quiet. He hadn't said anything since introducing her to one of his brothers. She believed his name was Leland, but she wasn't one hundred percent sure. Noland crowded her brain twenty four seven.

"Noland, are you okay?"

"I'm fine, why do you ask?"

"You've been awfully quiet. That's not like you at all."

"I'm sorry; I'm a little preoccupied right now."

"Okay."

Noland was a lot occupied. He saw the way his brother was looking at Abigail. His brother was probably more her type than him. Everybody always went for Leland. Arriving home, Noland opened his door and didn't unlock her door. Walking around to get to her door, Noland saw her puzzled expression.

"What's wrong now Abigail?'

"I just thought you forgot about me."

"I can never forget about you. You occupy my mind a lot."

"You know you can call me Abbey. You don't have to keep calling me Abigail."

"I like your name."

"Really, back in elementary they used to call me a big gal."

"Why?"

"It's how my name is spelled. A b i g a i l. I used to cry all the time."

"I would never pick on you. Look at my name, no land. People would say the Snow family has plenty of land. Children are cruel and adults just don't make it any better."

"I know you are right. That's why when I have children, I'm going to teach them that if you can't say something nice don't say anything at all."

"Abbey, I had fun tonight. We should try to do this again sometime."

"I like the sound of that, goodnight Noland."

"Goodnight Abbey."

Noland knew he was giving her the silent treatment but he was not trying to. He was mad at himself for getting angry at the way Leland was looking at Abbey. It was not her fault that she was so attractive and guys were just staring at her. She did not even seem to realize her appeal.

?Eighteen?

Noland waited for his brother to call. He just knew that Leland was going to call and drill him about his date. After waiting for fifteen minutes and no call, Noland headed upstairs to his own bed. When he put Abbey next door to him it was so he could hear her the first night she was here. Now it was torture to know she was next door with only a door separating them. All he had to do was get up and open the door. Like how it was opening right now.

"Abbey, is everything okay?"

"Noland, I've somehow got my zipper stuck. I can't get it to go up or down. Can you help me?"

The zipper she was talking about started in the middle of her back and ended at her butt. His hand has been playing with it all night as they danced, he has been waiting to unzip it all night. Now it seems his wish has to come true, but he has to be a gentleman. Could he unzip her dress and let her leave his room untouched?

"Okay, I see what the problem is; some of your hair is caught up in the zipper. I'll do my best not to pull your hair out."

"It doesn't matter as long as I can get out of this dress."

"I got all your hair out of the zipper."

"Thank you Noland. I would have hated to lose this dress." Abbey stated before kissing him.

"Abbey, please don't get me wrong, I do want you but I want you to be sure. I don't do gratitude sex."

"I wasn't proposing sex. I was thanking you for rescuing my dress. Everything doesn't have to lead to sex; sometimes it can lead to comfort. Believe me if and when I want sex from you, you will know it." Abbey stated before slamming the door shut.

Noland stood there in shock. He couldn't do or say anything right after seeing his brother. Maybe a long cold shower will help his brain function properly.

?Nineteen?

Noland didn't see much of Abbey the next day. She only came down to get something to eat and then she went back to her room.

He had to come up with some way to make peace with her.

Knocking on her door, Noland was coaching himself.

"I wanted to see if you wanted to share some Chinese takeout and maybe watch a movie."

"I don't know, I have a lot to do and."

"I also want to talk to you about last night. Please, Abbey, I hate the fact that we are not talking and you seem to be walking on eggshells around me."

"Okay, Noland. I'll share the takeout and watch a movie, just to show no hard feelings."

Once they got settled on the couch, Noland pressed pause on the movie.

"Abbey, I want to apologize to you about last night. I am really attracted to you and you can really inflate and deflate a man's ego in two seconds flat."

"Noland I don't understand you, you keep sending me these different signals."

"I want to get to know you a lot better and I don't think sex should be the answer."

"Who said anything about us having sex?"

"We will be having sex make no mistake about it. I just don't want that to be the main focus."

"Don't you think you are a little too cocky?"

"Nope, see you already messed up by letting me know you are attracted to me. So I'm going to use that to my advantage."

"Really, you should never let someone else see your hand. They can counterattack your actions."

"You know what's in my hand, but you can't play my hand and yours at the same time. I can always lead with something lower and let you take the lead."

"That's true, but you might not like where I lead you to."

"See that's what you think."

"Can we just watch the movie already?"

?Twenty?

Noland was happier; their first Saturday together went well. Now all they have to do is get Sunday over with.

"Noland, I don't know what to wear. What should I be prepared for?"

"You will meet my dad and brothers. One of my brothers will ask if we are in a serious relationship. That's only because I have never brought anyone home before. You should wear something warm and comfortable. Some jeans, a sweater and a coat should be fine. It's colder up the mountains. Be prepared for some snow. If it snows a lot we will leave early so that we won't get stuck up there, because of all the snow."

"Do I need to bring anything with me?"

"Yes, your competitive streak. We play a lot of board and card games on Sundays. Now hurry up or we'll be late."

"Do you have a coat that I can borrow? I haven't been able to find one that I liked, yet."

"Yes, and I see that we will be going shopping tomorrow morning. Don't say anything. We are getting you a coat that's practical. I don't care how the coat looks as long as it keeps you warm."

Abbey couldn't think of anything to say, so she stayed quiet. All she could think about was how she loved a man who opened the doors for her.

On the drive to his parents' house, Abbey asked him to tell her about his family.

He told her that his older brother, Damien, was the true rancher.

"His love for the land is evident in everything he does. After me, you have Leland, you meet him on Friday. He's a lawyer; he does work in Snowmass Village and Glenwood Springs. Then there's Calvin. He's one of the city councilmen for Glenwood Springs. After Calvin, there's Quincy, he's an accountant. Last but not least the triplets."

"Triplets, your parents have triplets?"

"Yes, they were trying for a girl, so I'm told. Darian, Adrian and Radian, are their names. Radian is a sheriff for Snowmass Village, Darian is a pilot for some private corporation and Adrian hasn't found his calling yet. None of us is married or seeing anyone at the moment."

"So you were serious when you said that I'll be the only other female."

"Yes, my family moved here back in 1910 and have been here since. Other than Adrian, no one has ever lived in any other state other than Colorado. I've traveled to other places, but this has always been home."

"I've never been this far north before in my life. So seeing snow on my way up here was a great surprise to me. I had to keep telling myself not to freak out. Don't laugh at me, and don't give me that innocent look either. I saw the smirk on your face."

"I swear that I was not laughing at you, but with you. I would never laugh at you, only with you."

"You know what they say about never, right?"

"Yes, I do."

"Now finish telling me about your family history."

He told her that family land is smaller than it used to be. The family sold it off a little at a time. His brothers and he had their own ten acres, a piece that was left to them from their paternal grandfather.

"It must be nice to actually have something passed down through time."

"I guess it is okay. I'm not really into the land. I've offered it to Damien several times, because I know that I will not do anything with it."

"Really, I don't understand. You do not want to keep it to pass down to your children someday?"

"I have my house that I can leave to them, if I have any children. The house sits on a few acres."

"I know I want to leave my children something if I ever have any."

"We are almost there."

Abbey was greatly surprised when they did arrive. He made the family home sound small. It was huge. The acres he talked about that they had a piece didn't even include what the house sat on or what was used for ranching. After Abbey got over her initial shock of the land and house she quite enjoyed herself.

She could see where Noland got his looks Damien Sr. was a great looking man. He had to be overly handsome in his younger days. Whatever woman that got Noland would forever look at him and smile, knowing she got a very handsome guy. Just thinking about some other woman being with him made her extremely angry. She couldn't believe that she was getting jealous of an imaginary woman. When did she start to care for him too much? Right then and there she decided that she needed to build a stronger brick wall around her heart.

That night when they arrived back at Noland's house there was a message from the doctor. He apologized, but he was extending his vacation for another week.

?Twenty One?

Noland wasn't looking forward to the doctor's visit the next day anyway. He had gotten used to coming home and seeing Abbey. She would have dinner ready. The house would be clean, not that it wasn't clean before her, it just had that extra shine and clean smell to it. It was truly amazing what someone could get used to in two weeks. He couldn't believe that it has only been two weeks. He was hoping that when they got home yesterday that the doctor had called and stated that he was going to stay another week, but no such luck. He didn't want to see Abbey go. Maybe, just maybe, he could convince her to stay here and not check into a hotel. It would be a lot cheaper on her and her client if she stayed with him. Plus, they have been getting along very well.

Abbey was sitting at the table with her own dilemma. She was excited about the doctor's visit today. She knew he would give her a clean bill of health. She didn't even have sniffles. She enjoyed being with Noland and that was her biggest problem. She was enjoying herself too much. He was everything that she ever wanted in a man. She couldn't believe she thought that jerk of a fiancé she had was the one. He wasn't even close, and she sees that now.

Abbey also realized that she was a fool for thinking that she could build a brick around her heart. Without even trying, Noland was slowly tearing down each brick she put up.

Every day, he would ask her how her day went. Was she any closer to finding out what she needed for her client? It was like he could read her mind. He knew exactly what to say or what she needed. Whether it was a shoulder massage, cooking dinner or ordering take out or bringing home some flowers he would surprise her at every turn. If she didn't know any better she would say that he was courting her. She could see that he was thinking real hard. It was in the way he held his lip.

"Abbey, I know and you know that the doctor is going to give you a clean bill of health. We have gotten along very well these past weeks. You could just stay here instead of checking into a hotel. It will help with the expenses. That will be one less thing that you will have to worry about trying to get from your client."

"Don't you think that I have imposed on you enough?"

"Imposed, I don't think having you here is imposing on anything. Have I complained to you about your being here? No, I didn't think so. I have enjoyed your company. Yes, I can admit that I have enjoyed it more than I thought I would. You don't have to give me an answer right now. I have taken off today, and you need a day off too. We can spend the day outside in the snow. After that we can go out to eat wherever you would like to go. I'll give you a real Colorado welcome."

"Okay, Noland, I will take the day off and spend some time with you. Tonight I will give you my decision on whether I will stay here or go to the hotel. Just promise me that you will not pressure me in any way."

"You have my word that I will not pressure you about staying." He stated as he got up to go answer the door bell.

?Twenty Two?

As they both predicted, the doctor said she was fit to leave.

They both were dressed in jogging suits with mittens, scarves and hats. Noland gave her a tour of his backyard. He had a good foot of snow in the back. He kept his front yard shoveled.

Abbey was overwhelmed with the size of his land. He said he had a few acres and she learned that a few was an understatement. The first thing they did was build a snow family. Then he took her sledding. He told her that whenever she wanted to he would take her skiing or snowboarding.

Abbey was having fun with the sledding, but that was not what she wanted to do in the snow.

"Noland, can we make some snow angels?"

"You want to make snow angels?"

"Yes, I've seen a lot of movies that show children making snow angels and I want to try it at least once."

"Okay, I know the perfect spot to make snow angels and then we can go inside and change."

"You are willing to make snow angels with me? Not just watch me make my own angels?"

"I'm willing to do anything that will make you happy."

"You know how to say the sweetest things."

"I know that you are away from home and Christmas is right around the corner."

"I haven't even thought about Christmas. That's easy to do when your house isn't decorated."

"I hadn't thought about it, that's all. You want to put up some Christmas decorations? We can go out today and buy some."

"Let me think about it first. I don't want to make any changes that you are not willing or have not thought of doing."

"I have already told you I just want to make you happy."

"Why do you want to make me happy?"

"I like the way your eyes light you when you truly smile. It is something very special to look at."

Abbey just glanced at him with a genuine smile. She was having too much fun playing in the snow.

Her incredible snowman was making a snow angel with her with his eyes closed. Sitting up, Abbey had a very sneaky idea. How long would it take for him to register that she hit him in the face with a snowball? Would she have enough time to make it inside the house before he retaliated? There was on one way to find out, she thought as she scooped up several handfuls of snow.

Noland was thinking how did he manage to tell her that he cared about her happiness? He had no plans on voicing that right now. He was beating himself up inside his mind. She had caught on to his mistake too. He was able to tell her some of the truth, but if he told her the whole truth she would up and leave. Run for the hills and never look back. He knew he had to have a serious talk with his dad. He wanted to ask his dad what were the clues to knowing the woman in your life was the one? They all knew that their parents had met and got married within two months of meeting each other. What they weren't sure of was how their parents knew that they wanted to spend the rest of their lives together? When they asked when they were young, their father said when you get older I will tell you.

Hell, he was older now and wanted to know for sure.

"Abbey, are you ready to go inside now or do you want to do something else first?"

"Do something else."

"What would you like to do?"

Before Noland could sit up and open his eyes, he was hit in the face with a giant snowball. He was in total shock for a full minute. After clearing off his face, he saw Abbey making a mad dash for the house. Grabbing two handfuls of snow as he was getting up, he went after her.

Abbey was laughing so hard that she had to stop and catch her breath. That short pause allowed Noland to catch up with her.

"Noland, I am so sorry."

"Really, I can't tell that you are, since you are laughing so hard."

"You should have seen your face. The look of total shock was written all over it." Abbey stated between breaths of laughter.

"I can't wait for your look of surprise."

"What are you talking about?" Abbey asked as she inched slowly away from him. She looked behind her and saw that she still had a great distance to go before making it to the house.

"Don't give me that you wouldn't dare look. We Snow men are known for our fairness towards both sexes. You may start the war, but we aim to either win or even the odds."

"Even the odds, how are you going to even the odds?"

"I'm so glad you asked." Then he proceeded to dump both handfuls of snow down the back of her shirt.

Abbey screamed so loud, he was glad that he didn't have any neighbors. If he did they would have called 911 on him. Now that was something to laugh at. He was too busy laughing to notice Abbey's stance. Abbey football tackled him and knocked him on his butt and the wind out of him.

"I see you forgot that I grew up with two brothers." She stated as she scooped up snow and put it down his shirt, all over his neck and face, while straddling him.

Noland couldn't say which surprised him more, her strength or the fact that she was on him. He better do something quick before she found out how much he really enjoyed this position.

?Twenty Three?

Noland grabbed her hands and sat up.

"Okay, you win Abbey. I know when I've been bested. Just promise me you will not tell a soul."

"I can't promise you that."

"Just promise you won't tell my brothers."

"I might be able to do that if we can come to an agreement of some sorts."

"I should have known there was a little devil in you somewhere. As much as I would love to debate with you, I am sitting in the snow. My butt has gone quite numb from the snow."

"I do apologize for that. Did I hurt you?"

"Only my pride, you are the first female that has been able to put me on my butt. Come on, let's go inside and change clothes." The snow did nothing for his libido.

Every time they touched, there was an electricity surge that went through him. There's a very strong sexual surge that he had to fight whenever it happened. He has gotten better with being in her company and not acting on his first instinct to kiss her. He had to lie to her, well actually most of it was true, to get her off him, just now. If he hadn't they would be in the snow right now making out. Their first time was going to be in a bed, his bed at that. Not in the snow or on his kitchen counter. Whenever he was around her he acted like some lusty teenager.

Abbey knew for a fact that Noland was going to kiss her. She could see it in his eyes. If he would have, she would have been powerless to do anything about it. She longed for his kisses, but she wasn't going to tell him that. She was a little disappointed when he didn't. Abbey needed to stay on track and she was glad Noland was helping her do that.

"What would you like to eat tonight?"

"I was thinking about some pizza. I haven't had any type of pizza since I've been here."

"Then pizza it is. I'll order the pizza you go ahead and take a shower. It should be here in about forty-five minutes."

Noland ordered two large pizzas. One was supreme and the other was meat lovers. As he slowly ascended the stairs, he knew his shower was going to be a nice frigid one. Even cold showers had started to lose their power. How many more would he have to take?

?Twenty Four?

Noland was already downstairs and setting up the living room, when Abbey came down. He had paper plates, napkins and paper cups. She could see a stack of movies sitting in between the plates.

"I figured we could watch some movies. I wasn't sure what you like. So I got a few dramas, love stories and action movies."

"I like all kinds of movies, but I love thrillers the best."

"Have a seat and look over the movies. The pizza should be here soon."

"Am I going to like the pizza you ordered?"

"I hope so, I ordered two different types."

"Well, I know for sure one of them is going to be something with a lot of meat."

"So, you have seen my freezer."

"A person who knows what they like is a plus in anybody's book or should be at least."

"You are a plus in my book. You go after what you want and I've noticed that you have a thing for purple."

"I don't always go after something I want. I love purple, but how do you know I have a thing for purple?"

Noland didn't get the chance to answer her question. He was saved by the bell so to speak. After paying the delivery guy, Noland turned to find Abbey patiently waiting for him to answer her question.

"I know you have a thing for purple simply by all those purple bags I had to carry in."

"Oh."

?Twenty Five?

Noland was puzzled with her statement of "Oh", but he let it go.

"What movie did you decide on?"

"I'm stuck between *Premonition* and *Déjà Vu*. They both sound good."

"Let's watch *Déjà Vu* first then after that we will watch *Premonition*."

"Noland, I want to ask you a serious question."

"Okay, I just might answer your serious question if I get to ask one of my own."

"Deal, I want to know why aren't you married or at least in a serious relationship?"

"I haven't met anyone who grabbed my attention before you. I want the type of love my parents have. My parents are a distraction to each other and that's what I want."

"So you are saying I'm a distraction?"

"You're the best and most distraction I've had in my whole life. Now for my question, why aren't you married?"

"Do you really want to know?" Seeing that he wasn't going to answer her question she went on.

"It's not that I wasn't in a relationship. I was but the relationship was one sided. I thought I loved him and thought he loved me. I was supposed to get married last month, but instead of the wedding announcement in the paper there was a departing announcement."

"A departing announcement, explain that one to me?"

"He worked for the newspaper; *Miami Tribute*. It's the hottest and most read newspaper in Florida. I had a business partner who always tried to convince me that I needed to be a little thinner. He left me for my skinny business partner, and took off for parts unknown. They were dating the whole time. It was a big ugly mess of an announcement."

"How hurtful was it?"

"Well, he didn't break my heart, but I thought I was content with him. There were some words that were more hurtful than the fact that he was leaving or the fact that he did it the way he did."

"Words like what?"

"Noland, it doesn't matter."

"Yes, it does. If it bothers you it bothers me."

"Why? Noland I don't understand why it should bother you?"

"I like to see you happy. I could have sworn that I told you this already. I love the way you smile, I never want to see you hurt."

"I was called fat because I had too much meat on my bones and no kind of guy would ever want me. Are you happy now?"

"No. You are not fat, and no I am not happy. I really like your body shape. If it's not every man's dream it is most definitely my dream body."

Noland leaned over and kissed Abbey before she could say anything. It was the only way he could show her that they were wrong. He wanted her more than he could say. So he figured showing her was easier.

"Noland, what are you doing?"

"I'm showing you that your ex was a jerk, and that he doesn't know anything about a woman."

"So you are giving me a pity kiss?"

"No, I'm giving you that I want you so badly right now kiss."

Before she could say something else crazy, Noland started kissing her again. What he couldn't understand is why she had on this long t-shirt. Pulling up her t-shirt he came across another shirt.

"Why do you have so many shirts on?"

"I only wear another shirt around you."

"Let's take this one off." He stated right before pulling it over her head. The shirt she had on underneath was pure sexy, now he understood why. It was one of those shelf camisole shirts.

"Damn, you just take my breath away."

Abbey saw the flash of desire in his eyes before he started kissing her again. Okay desire was not the word for what she saw. There were too many emotions and she just couldn't put a finger on what to call it.

As soon as Noland touched her breast all of her thoughts flew out the window. All she could think about was getting closer.

Abbey's moan was all the encouragement that he needed. Letting go of her lips, Noland trailed kisses down her throat to her collarbone. Pull the straps down on her shirt to free her breasts all he could do was stare at them. They weren't small but not huge either. Her breasts were just a little more than a handful.

"You have an incredible body."

"Thank you. Now take off your shirt."

"No, I was thinking more on the lines of you taking off my shirt."

Abbey sat up and pulled her shirt over her head and threw it on the table. Reaching over she slowly pulled Noland's shirt up. With every inch she showed she gave his stomach a kiss. He had this amazing stomach. It was not a washboard stomach but hell it was still sexy. She loved the way his nerves jumped every time she kissed a new spot. When his shirt was finally over his head Abbey started kissing him.

Sliding her hands down his chest and stomach, she had a destination in mind, getting him out of his pants.

When her right hand touched him, Noland knew he no longer had control of the situation. All he could do was lift up so she could pull his pants down. Trailing kisses down his neck and giving soft bites on him, Abbey knew that this was not her. She never took control of sex. Noland just brought out the desire in her.

Noland slid her pants and panties off her body. He had to have her now. The bed had to wait for another time. Pulling her over him, he made Abbey straddle him. The surprise look on her face said it all.

"We will go at your pace."

Abbey slowly lowered herself on him. She was more than ready for him, but a little scared because she has never been on top. At Noland groans, Abbey knew she had to be doing something right. She rose up slowly and lowered herself all the way this time on him.

"Damn, Abbey I know I said we will go at your pace, but you are killing me. I mean that in a good way." Noland stated when she continued to go at a slow pace.

Abbey knew what he meant because she was killing herself too. It felt so good to be in control of everything. Noland touched places in her that she didn't know existed. He filled her to the hilt and it was driving her crazy.

His hands were everywhere on her body, but he was true to his word, they went at her pace. He could tell she was made just for him. Her body proportion and the way she fit him like a glove.

"Noland, I can't, I'm about to."

"Just let it go."

Watching Abbey reach her climax, he couldn't hold back his own.

"Wow, oh my, Noland that was. I have never. That has never."

"Abbey, are you okay?" He was a little concerned, since she couldn't complete her sentences.

Abbey was in total shock. This was the first time she had an orgasm during sex ever.

"Abbey, are you okay?"

"Yes, I'm better than okay. I'm sorry I just had a lot going on inside my head, that's all."

"Do you want to finish the movie or go upstairs?"

"Can I sit here a bit or am I hurting you?"

"We can sit here as long as you like, but I must warn you. If we sit here too long there will be a round two."

"I like the sound of that." Then she started biting his neck again.

"That does it, we are going upstairs."

Noland stood straight up and walked toward the stairs.

"Put me down."

"I will as soon as we get to my bed."

"I know that I'm too heavy for you."

"No you are not. All I need from you is to wrap your legs around me. It will make going up the stairs easier."

Abbey stopped complaining and did as he wished. With each step he took up the stairs was a tease to her lower region. By the time he laid her on the bed, she was almost at the peak again.

Noland slipped inside her slowly. He wanted to savor the feeling of being inside her. It wasn't too long before she crossed the crest that he had her dangling at and he was right behind her.

"Again, I can't believe it happened again."

"Can't believe what happened again?"

"Did I say that out loud?"

"Yes you did and I'm still waiting for an answer."

Embarrassed by what she said Abbey just shook her head. She wasn't about to admit that to him.

"Abbey..."

"Noland, just leave it alone for now. I need to sort it out for myself first."

She wasn't about to tell him right now that he was the first guy to ever give her an orgasm during sex. It was bad enough that he gave her the first one, but two in less than an hour.

Noland repositioned himself so that they were in the spoon position.

?Twenty Six?

As soon as her body relaxed and her breathing even out, Noland got up and went downstairs. He stared at the blank television for a long time. He had so much on his mind. He could not believe what just happened. He really wanted to know what she was talking about. So he knew for a fact that he was way past caring for her phase. He was trying to figure out when he fell in love with her. Hearing a noise behind him, Noland glanced at the clock and was surprised that it was an hour later. He turned around to see Abbey coming down the stairs with the sheet wrapped around her.

"Are you okay?"

"Yeah, I'm okay Abbey."

With a nod she started to clean up the food they completely forgot about.

"You don't have to do that, you know."

"I know but I don't mind."

After she cleared the trash away there was still that long eerie silence. She sat on the couch beside him.

"Do you want me to leave?"

"No! Why would I want you to leave?"

"You seem so distant and moody. This is the second time you have been this quiet. The first time we had a slight disagreement. I thought maybe you regretted it."

"No, I don't regret it. The only thing I regret is that you have to go back home some time."

"It's taking a little longer to get anywhere with the lawyer. So if my client wants me to stay longer I will be here longer."

"It's still temporary." Picking up his discarded clothes he started putting them on.

"You're leaving?"

"I'll be back. I need to clear my head and go see my dad about a few things. This has nothing to do with what just happened." He kissed her fully on the lips and walked to the door.

Abbey just stood there staring at the closed door. His leaving really caught her off guard. Twice he just simply left her. How can he tell her that it had nothing to do with her and she knew it had everything to do with her? She picked up her scattered clothing and went to the room she's been using since she's been here. After sitting on the bed and trying to work out her feelings she called her best friend. Katriel knew everything about her and she would advise her on the best next move.

When Noland arrived at his parent's house, he went to the work room that was in the back. His father converted the guest house into the work room when all of them moved out.

"Hi, Dad, how are you doing today?"

"Hi Noland, I'm doing well. So what can I help you with today?"

"Remember when we were young and you told us when we get older you would tell us how we would know if it was true love?"

"Well it took you long enough?"

"Took me long enough? What are you talking about? Damien is the oldest shouldn't he feel the pressure first?"

"Nobody's pressuring anybody. I simply meant it took you long enough to realize that you are in love with Abbey."

"Took me long enough to realize?"

"Everybody could tell that you were in love with her. Of course Leland knew the first night he saw you at the club with her. It's easy for an onlooker to spot, before the person. You are the most relaxed I have ever seen you and I know it's all because of Abbey. When the woman you are with makes you forget that you have to work in the morning or make you wish you didn't, and then she is the one for you."

"I can't just expect her to give up her life in Miami and I can't give up what I have here."

"Material things should not be that important. Plus, how do you know if she's willing to give it up or not? Did you already ask her?"

"No, I haven't talked to her about how I think I feel."

"Why the hell not, Noland, what are you thinking?" Damien asked.

"It's too soon. I haven't known her long enough."

"Only long enough to get her in your bed, right?"

"I didn't say anything to you about that."

"You didn't have too. You have bite marks all over your neck. You are here having a serious conversation about being in love with her. Love at first sight does exist but it doesn't always work out. Yours will be at a cost. Now go home and tell her how you feel before it's too late to undo the damage you have caused."

"Damage, what damage?"

"You are here talking to me and not her. Abandoning her this quickly after sex is not a good sign on your part. Conversation is the key in any type of relationship."

"Shit."

"Hey, watch your language."

"Sorry, kiss mom for me."

"Is that Noland I see running away?"

"Yep, he came here to ask about love."

"Some of you men are slow on that, but I was hoping Noland was different."

"Slow. That's not the only thing we are slow at. Come on, let me show you another way we are slow."

"See this is how we ended up with eight children."

?Twenty Seven?

When Noland arrived home Abbey was not there. He knew she didn't leave for the hotel or Miami because her clothes were still in the closet. Yes, it was pathetic that he checked to make sure that she was still going to be at the house. Maybe she was driving around town or just went somewhere to cool off. After his talk with his father, he realized leaving was not his best action. He couldn't call her because he didn't have her cell number.

After three hours of endless waiting, worrying, and pacing he finally heard the key unlock the door. She walked in on the phone but Noland was past the point of caring.

"Where the hell have you been? I've been worried sick. Did you know that I don't even have your cell number?"

"Yeah, I know right. Let me call you back tomorrow. I have to handle this quickly. Okay bye." Abbey's facial expression changed by the time she looked at Noland.

"Well, I'm waiting."

"Your point in this whole matter is?"

"You don't just leave without a note or a call saying you're going to be gone for a while."

"Funny Noland you don't look Irish to me."

"Irish, what do being Irish have to do with it?"

"Yes, Irish. The only man that can demand an answer from me is Irish. When I graduated from high school he stopped demanding and started asking."

Thrown for a loop all Noland could do was stand there and stare.

"Your dad's Irish?"

"Yes, that's how I have red hair and green eyes."

"Your skin isn't pale. Most redheads have pale skin."

"That's because my mom isn't Irish."

"What is your mom?"

"What is it to you?"

"I would like to know more about you."

"Simply because we had sex doesn't mean that I'm going to tell you everything about my life."

"We need to talk about that."

"By saying that I assume you mean sex. That's all it was, sex and there's nothing else to talk about."

"Yes there is. I just wanted you to know that I."

"Noland save your sob stories and excuses for another woman."

"I need you to listen to what I have to say."

"What I'm going to do is head to bed. I have a long pressing day ahead of me. Good night."

Noland saw her fiery temper come to the surface and knew this was the wrong time to try to talk to her about love. His dad was right he did a lot of damage and now he was going to have to find a way to fix the damage.

?Twenty Eight?

For the next three days, Noland only saw a few flashes of Abbey. The only reason why is because he would go to her room and make sure she was still there. She would be sound asleep when he left for work and was never home when he got in. She came in late at night and would be on her phone when she did come in.

Christmas was three weeks away. He wasn't worried about her not showing up at his parents' house. On Sunday, she was at her best. You wouldn't even know that they weren't talking to each other.

She always came in early on a Friday, so tonight he was in the kitchen cooking dinner. He was pulling out all the stops to get her attention.

When Abbey came in she noticed that there was some soft jazz music playing. The music was so relaxing after a tiring day. What she couldn't understand was why Leland was being so difficult. With her bags still on her shoulder, she just plopped down on the couch and closed her eyes. She was not sure how long she sat there like that, but when she opened her eyes she saw Noland. He was sitting besides her nudging her awake.

"How long have I been asleep?"

"I would say about an hour. Do you want me to help you get in the bed or would you like to eat first?"

Before she could decline both offers her stomach growled.

"Well, I guess that answers my question. Come on, I have already set the table."

Seeing that she couldn't refuse without looking crazy she followed him to the table. She was glad that she went to the table to eat. She hadn't realized how many meals she had skipped, or how much she missed it being just Noland and her.

"Abbey, why are you avoiding being in my presence?" Noland asked after they were done eating.

"Noland as much as I would like to be avoiding you because of my pride, I'm not. The one person I need to see the most to help with my investigation has a very busy schedule and there's a lot of paperwork to sort through."

"The one thing you are not is a good liar."

"Truthfully, at first I was trying to avoid you, but now it's uneventful. I just can't seem to catch the one person I need to talk to. I'm at a standstill. I feel like a failure."

"You are not a failure." Noland said as he pulled her into his arms.

He felt a strong desire run through him, but at this moment that was not what she needed. He knew she needed to be protected and helped and that's all he was offering. He knew if he voiced how he felt about her that would break the spell. Abbey was a strong determined woman, his strong determined woman.

?Twenty Nine?

Noland was only going to comfort her, but her sigh made him forget about comforting her. Having her in his arms was both pleasure and torture. He moaned out her name because he didn't know what else to do. When she looked up at him he knew he lost the battle without putting up much of a fight. He had to kiss her without scaring her.

Hearing Noland moan her name, Abbey glanced up. She knew looking at him would be a mistake but she couldn't help herself. The moment she finished lifting her head to look at him, she saw his lips slowly descending toward her. She had plenty of time to stop the kiss, but she didn't have the power, strength, or desire to stop it. His lips were barely touching her lips. It was the softest kiss she ever had in her life. It wasn't demanding but at the same time it was very demanding. She could feel compassion, desire and something she could not quite put her finger on.

"Noland, please I." Abbey whispered against his lips.

"Please, what Abbey?" He was confused. Did she want him to continue or stop? He believed he could stop if he had to, but he really didn't want to. When she didn't respond he asked, "Do you want me to stop or keep going?"

"I want you to keep going."

Noland didn't realize he was holding his breath until it came out as a big whoosh at her answer. Sweeping her up into his arms, Noland took the steps two at a time. He put her down beside his bed, still not sure if this was what she wanted. Abbey noticed his hesitation and gave a shy smile. She pulled his head toward her and lightly bit his lip and then she slowly licked the area she offended. Noland moaned and sought out her tongue with his. When their tongues touched for the first time in weeks, they both groaned out loud. Their lips only parted twice, when she took off their clothes and when they fell back into bed.

"Abbey, was I too rough or did I hurt you at all?" Noland asked once he was able to find his voice. He lost control of himself as soon as they hit the bed.

"Hmm!" Abbey said, stretching lazily. "No you didn't hurt me and you weren't rough either. You were incredible. I got my own incredible Snowman."

Before he could say anything else he heard a soft snore.

"Well I guess that's my cue to go clean up downstairs." He said out loud to no one in particular. He pulled on his pants that were thrown across the room.

After he finished loading the dishwasher, his cell phone ranged. It was Lily calling to let him know that someone needed to get their car out of a ditch. The ditch accident happened because they swerved to avoid hitting an animal. For the first time ever, he told her to call Earl and have him deal with it. Smiling Noland settled down behind Abbey and pulled her closer in his embrace, before joining her in dreamland.

?Thirty?

Abbey woke up disoriented the next morning. All she knew was that she had a very peaceful sleep and she couldn't move for any reason. There was something very heavy pinning her down. Looking down at the arm that was holding her down, she couldn't believe it. This was the first time she slept in the bed with a guy. Removing his arm from around her she went to the room she was currently using to think. She couldn't have been in there for more than five minutes before she saw Noland standing at the door.

"Are you okay, Abbey?" Seeing her expression he knew she was wondering how he knew she was gone. "I woke up as soon as you moved my arm from around you. I just thought you were going to the restroom, but you were gone a little too long, and I didn't hear any water running."

"I'm not sure what I'm doing here. I'm so out of my element with you. You are a big distraction, Noland and I am not sure if I can afford that right now. I have a job to finish and it's already hard trying to see the lawyer I need to see to get all the information I need."

"Is this explanation your way of asking for space?"

"I don't want space, I am not sure what I want or need at this moment. I'm so confused."

"I promise you that I will not pressure you. If you start to feel smothered just let me know and I'll back off. I promise. You're my distraction too, so we are in the same boat."

After that morning's conversation Noland and Abbey had fallen into a routine for the next few weeks. Abbey would come in before five and they would have dinner together. Noland had invited her to lunch a couple of times but she refused because she didn't want to go to his shop. She still didn't like his receptionist, but she was not going to cause the woman to lose her job.

?Thirty One?

Abbey kept in touch with Marilyn every day. Letting her know that she still couldn't get past Leland, Noland's brother, to see the attorney who sent her the letter. Abbey was hoping to have this wrapped up before Christmas. Christmas was just two days away and she was still at a standstill. Leland told her that after the New Year he would give her the documents that Marilyn had to fill out and bring back in person. Every day for two weeks she would be outside the coffee shop that Leland would visit trying to persuade him to give her the information sooner, so she could get her job over with. Every day he would tell her the same thing. Not to worry, the papers will be ready in the New Year.

Today was the same thing, but a little different.

"Abbey, every day we go through the same thing. Every day I tell you the same thing. The office is officially closed; it will not open again until January 2nd. This is the reason why the papers will not be ready until after the New Year. So let's have a peaceful Christmas and New Year please. I promise you first thing on January 2nd, I will hand you the documents you need to send with the postage to have them sent to Marilyn. Now go home and get some rest please."

"Leland, you know you are not right. I could have finished this whole project a month ago, why are you delaying it."

"Aren't you enjoying spending time with my brother? So what's the hurry and harm in me taking my time? Plus we were hoping to see Marilyn, not a private investigator."

"I'm here to ensure that the information is true and that no one is trying to string my client alone in a money scam. She has had enough of this, maybe your mother crap."

"You make it sound a little too personal."

"It is why I have to waste my time and my client's money chasing after this, maybe your mother."

"I promise you this is not a scam. Now go home and get some rest."

Neither one of them saw Lily watching them hug and part ways.

Lily was wishing she had a camera so she could show her boss that the woman he was crazy over was playing his brother and him. She still couldn't see what either one of them saw in a fat woman like her.

?Thirty Two?

With their new routine, Noland and Abbey slept every night in the same bed. To Abbey it was very shocking to enjoy waking up in a man's arms.

"Good morning, beautiful."

"Good morning, handsome. It's Christmas Eve, can you believe it?"

"I'm going to need you to pack an overnight bag." At her confused look, he continued. "We are going to my parents for Christmas's Eve dinner and to open presents on Christmas Day."

"I haven't bought anybody anything for Christmas. I can't go there empty handed."

"You have already bought the presents, you just didn't know it."

"Really, you bought the presents and just had my name added on to them?"

"Yes, now get up and go do as I ask. It's not a demand, it's a request with firmness." At her hesitation he added. "I know you are not trying to play the shy role. I have seen your body before we had sex."

"Yes, I remember but this is a first for me."

"What's a first for you?"

"Waking you in some guy's bed is a first for me."

"Now I'm just some guy."

"You know what I mean. I know we have been sleeping in the same bed every night, by the time I get up you have already left for work. I was with my ex but I never spent the night or vice versa."

"Well I can think of other things we could be doing right now. We'll be late and everyone will know why we are late."

Abbey jumped out of the bed and ran to the other room.

Noland chuckled, he knew that his parents knew they were having sex but his brothers kept asking and he wasn't telling. While she was in the shower, Noland called Damien.

"Are you still having problems with the Frost Company?"

"Sorry about the hello I gave. Yes, she had the nerve to call me this morning. It's a holiday and a weekend. I don't see why that man just won't let the place be until the New Year. To have his secretary work on the weekend and a holiday is crazy."

"I don't understand why you keep answering the phone when you see the number come up."

"She has a nice voice."

"Who has a nice voice, the secretary?"

"Yes it's so sexy and I like the way it hitches up when she gets angry. I wonder if he takes her to any of his business meetings."

"You are crazy. Did you get mom to air out the guest room?"

"Yeah, she wasn't too happy about it either. If you want my opinion?"

"I don't want it."

"I'm going to give it to you anyway, since I'm the oldest. You should be sleeping with her by now. I don't understand, she's very beautiful and that body she has is totally awesome. You've been cohabiting for over two months now. Hell, cohabiting for twenty days is too long."

"I know you are my older brother, but I don't need you giving me any type of advice, especially when you are still single yourself. Plus your way of thinking is the reason why you are still single, living at home with mom and dad."

"That was a low blow; you know I have my own house on my land. I will see you when you get here."

Halfway to his parents' house Abbey turned toward Noland. He hadn't said anything about their sleeping situation at his parents' house.

"Are you going to be sleeping in the same bed at, your parents?"

"No, to Mom's biggest disappointment I had her air out the guest room. I didn't want my brothers to know."

"Good I don't want to give them the wrong impression about me."

"That you could be lusting after my body more than you let on?"

"No, that I'm having a fling with you."

Noland could not say anything to that because he was trying to figure out what they were having. Is this all that it is a fling? Is that how she saw it? He knew he had fallen in love with her, but she was a practical woman. She didn't believe in love at first sight.

At dinner, Abbey could tell that there was something wrong with Noland. He had been withdrawn since she admitted that she was having a fling with him. She could not understand why he was upset about it. It's not a relationship since there is no commitment involved. She could not classify it as a one night stand. Okay maybe she could have used a different word for it but love affair is not what she would call it since love was never said. She didn't know what she felt for him.

?Thirty Three?

On Christmas morning, Abbey called her family and friends to wish them a Merry Christmas. She let them know she will be returning back home as soon as she could. For breakfast it was quite plentiful since there was not going to be any lunch. Lunch time was for opening presents, which Abbey had more presents than she thought she would have. The one present she wanted, she did not get from Leland and that was Marilyn's birth records or at least an appointment to see the lawyer.

She had the most romantic date she ever had on New Year's Eve. She went to the family's ski lodge, which Damien somewhat ran. There was skiing, hot chocolate, exotic massages and a lot of tenderness going on. She knew her heart was in trouble. When they made love, it was different than the other times. It was more heartfelt. When Abbey reached her climax, she was speechless with tears in her eyes. The tears ran down her face.

Noland saw the tears. "Abbey, did I hurt you?"

Abbey just shook her head no. She was unable to voice the tenderness and unsuppressed emotions that passed through her. How could she explain it to him, when she could not understand it herself?

The next day it was back to work. Abbey walked out of the bathroom with the towel wrapped around her. Noland was lying in bed watching her. Noland called her name and then got out of the bed and approached her.

"Noland, don't you have to be at work?"

"Work can wait, having you right now cannot." Pulling her to him, he made sure that the hardest part of him came in contact with the softest part of her. That brief contact made all the rebuttals fly out of her head.

"I have to taste you before I go to work." He whispered against her ear, sending shivers down her spine. Then he started licking the most sensitive part of her neck. Abbey would have fallen if it wasn't for him holding her hips. She had never met a man who made her feel so wanton. Was she a floozy, for letting him turn her on so quickly, not that she could help it?

Later on that day while at work all Noland could think about was earlier. He enjoyed the way Abbey moaned his name. Just thinking about it made him want to find her and repeat the experience. It was a good thing he was under the car.

"Noland, you have a phone call."

"Please take a message, Lily. I need to finish this car today."

"It's that woman!"

Rolling his head from underneath the car, he had a confused look on his face. "Who's that woman? Do you have a problem with one of our customers? If so, I can talk to them and find out what happened."

"It's not a customer. It's her! I know you really like her, but I have seen her in town with another guy. I don't think it's right at all, but it's none of my business." She thrust one of the cordless phones at him and walked away. Of course, the conversation cooled down his heated body quickly.

"Hello."

"Noland, sorry to be calling you while you are at work but I think that my battery is dead. Can you come and give me a jump start?"

"Yes I can swing by and help you out. Where are you now?"

"I'm parked in the library parking lot."

"Okay, I'll be there shortly."

?Thirty Four?

Noland could not believe that Lily had a problem with Abbey. Plus, he wanted to know what this business is about Abbey and another guy? When he walked in the office, Lily was on the phone, so he just walked out. He got to the library and saw Abbey passing back and forth in front of her car. He pulled up beside her and he saw that she was extremely happy to see him. Her battery was fine; she just had a few loose cables under the hood.

"Will you come home early tonight?"

"I really hope so, Noland. Things are not going the way I hoped they would today."

"We are going to have a sit down talk. I need to find out a few things from you."

"Okay, I'll be there."

After her agreement, Noland kissed her on the lips and left.

Abbey went straight to the house after Noland fixed her car. She cleaned up the house and thought about starting dinner. Marilyn called before she could make up her mind. When Noland came in Abbey was still on the phone. He grabbed her and kissed her hard on the mouth.

"I have been thinking about you all day. I missed you."

Abbey stood there looking at him like he was crazy. Okay maybe he was a little crazy because he never showed her that much affection before. He also never said anything to her while she was on the phone either. He was still a little steamed about what Lily said.

"Look sweetie I was not ignoring you. No, I will not tell you who that was. I will not tell you because I know you all too well. No he is not important right now. I am doing the best I can right now. No, I did not break my promise. Yes, I do remember what I promised you. Look honey you sent me up here to do a job and I'm doing it. Just sign the damn paper work I sent you. I'm sorry I didn't mean to cuss. It took me forever to get that much from the lawyer. Thank you, goodnight." The whole time she was having the conversation, Noland was standing there watching her watch him.

"Tell me that you were talking to someone that is related to you?"

"No, it was not a relative I was talking to."

"Two more questions, then I'll let you finish." Noland said when he cut her off. "Why am I not important right now and what did you promise?"

"I would be on the phone forever explaining your presence, which ties in with what I promised. I promised that I would not come up here and fall in love with the first man I saw."

"Well I can see how that would really put things into perspective."

"Noland, wait, I can explain."

"Explain what? How you were able to keep your promise you made or why am I not important? What would you call this relationship that we are in?"

Abbey opened her mouth to explain but no words came out. She was trying to come to terms with what kind of relationship they were in. Truthfully she wouldn't be able to answer any of his questions.

"That does explain it all."

Abbey watches Noland walk out the door and slammed it with such a powerful force the house shook. She realized that she messed up big time. She wasn't in love with him, was she? She didn't believe in love at first sight. Abbey sunk down to the floor. She was totally in love with him. She wasn't even sure when it happened. She had to go; she couldn't let heart get broken.

Abbey was on the road in less than an hour heading back to Miami. She packed so fast that her arms were actually hurting. Of course, it could be that she was gripping the steering wheel so tight.

Noland never came home that night. He spent the next two days at Leland's house.

"You know being in a drunken stupor isn't going to make the pain go away."

"If I wanted advice I would have stayed over at Damien's."

"I'm just saying that this pain that you are feeling is not going to go away with drowning it in a drink."

"How do you know? Have you ever had the woman you love, yes love, tell you she's not in love with you?"

"Did she actually tell you that or the person she was on the phone with?"

"Isn't it the same thing?"

"No, it's not. You were listening to a one-sided conversation. She was trying to convince her friend, Marilyn, that she hadn't broken her promise, so she would not drive up here. Of course, Marilyn was not convinced."

"How do you know all this?"

"Abbey called me this morning and told me."

"What do you mean Abbey called you? Why the hell does she have your number?" Noland asked while interrupting his brother's story.

"It's nothing like that, Noland. I know better than to step into any of my brother's territory and try to take their woman."

"Well you better explain it to me and fast."

"She stopped in Atlanta to call her friends and one of them informed her that Marilyn was already on her way to Colorado."

"What do you mean by stopped in Atlanta?" Noland asked, sobering up a little.

"You know, Atlanta, Georgia. Some people do use Atlanta on their way to Florida."

"I know where Atlanta is."

"Then why did you ask?"

"Are you trying to tell me she left?"

"For a person who wants me to explain things to him you interrupt a lot."

"I'm asking questions to come to terms with all this now. Did she leave?"

"One thing is for sure, she is no longer here in this state or at your house."

"When did she leave?"

"I guess the same night you did. I didn't see her yesterday morning or this morning. I didn't think of it. Just thought she gave up until she called me to warn me about her friend named Marilyn."

"Given up on what?"

"Okay, every morning for the past two months, I see Abbey. Wait before you get it all wrong." Leland added when he saw his brother start to rise. "She was here to get her friend's family information."

"I take it you mean her friend's family information, you mean Marilyn."

"Yes, Marilyn's parents were the Campbell's' and I could not let her find out the gruesome details of what happened. It seems like I messed that up because now I have to deal with Marilyn and she's worse than Abbey. I met Marilyn this afternoon."

"You were the person giving her a hard time."

"I plead guilty to that statement, but I thought she told you. I made the mistake of giving her my cell phone number the day I saw her at the office. She would call me everyday harassing me for the adoption papers. Then she would come down to the office and harass me even more. I finally gave her some of the paper for Marilyn to fill out and return."

"Damn, she would not tell who the lawyer was. In a way I can understand why. She could have thought it would cause a conflict in the family. I wished she would have told me. I really blew up in her face after Lily told me that she had seen her with another guy."

"Come on Noland, you can't be that slow can you? Lily has had a huge crush on you since she was a freshman in high school. She always had and I reckon she always will until some other guy comes along."

"To be honest with you, Lily did tell the truth. Plus I thought Lily had a thing for you. It may have been from a person on the outside looking in, but it was the truth. She did see Abbey with another guy and a guy who just so happened to be my brother. She might have thought Abbey was playing us both. Now I have to see why Abbey left. I never gave her the chance to explain. I asked her compound questions. I got to get my things in order so I can go get her and allow her to explain things to me. Do you, by chance, happen to have her cell number?"

Leland said with a smile. "I thought you would never ask."

?Thirty Five?

It took Noland longer than expected to get everything in order. It actually took him two months to prepare his brother, Adrian, to get ready to manage the shop for him. He had a nice long chat with Lily, and found out that she did cause a lot of pain to Abbey. He got to meet both Marilyn and Jaclynn, which both of them gave him a piece of their mind and some advice. It was Marilyn who gave him Abbey's address and code to her gate. He really likes both of them especially since they both were driving two of his brothers crazy. It was fun to watch his brothers' jump through a few hurdles. After driving for ten hours he realized and wished that he had flown down to Miami. He preferred his own and that was the only reason why he drove. He was extremely glad when he pulled in front of her house. It put more pep in his step when he parked right behind her SUV.

"The door's open." Abbey responded he got after ringing the doorbell. So he walked in and got déjà vu.

Abbey was once again bent over with her head in the stove.

"I don't think I ever told you how much I like this view."

Noland was all she could get out after some of the shock wore off.

He walked up to her and trapped her by the stove. "Yeah, it's me." Then he lowered his lips to hers.

Abbey could taste hurt, anger and desire in his kiss. There was a hint of something else that she could not quite put her finger on. She was so consumed by an overwhelming need to become one with him that she stopped trying to figure out what the other emotion was. How could there still be so much fire? Didn't he go on with his life when he realized that she would not answer or return his calls?

"Young man, if you don't get your hands off my daughter. I'm going to make you wish you were never born.

Noland turned his head to see a very beautiful mocha colored woman. He could tell that she was Abbey's mom just by her build and some of her features. He turned his head and whispered to Abbey. "If I move your mom will see how much I want you."

"Mom, can you go and put those in my room, I will be there in a minute."

"Okay, young lady, but I expect you to explain to me about him and why he feels he has the right to kiss you."

"For some reason I don't have any kind of luck with you in the kitchen."

"You can sit down at the table and that's all the luck you will get from me. Now I have to go and explain who you are to my mom. When I return I expect you to explain to me why you are here."

Abbey walked into her room and shut the bedroom door. She wasn't ready for him to over hear anything that she wasn't quite ready to tell him.

"Mom, I can explain."

"You don't have to explain to me who he is. I have already gathered that he has to be Noland."

Abbey nodded her head. "I wasn't expecting him at all. I don't even know how he knew where I live. He just appeared out of the blue. I thought I was dreaming until he kissed me."

"I can tell you this much, he's quite handsome, looked happy to see you and you looked very happy to see him."

"He caught me off guard."

"Do you love him?"

"Yes I love him, but."

"There is no, buts. You either love him or you don't. If you do love him you need to tell him so and stop both of you from suffering. What I saw in that man's eyes when he looked at me was pain and love. You can stop this torture you both are going through."

"I don't think you saw love in his eyes. That had to be desire, he only desires me."

"No baby, I know love when I see it. Desire does not drive over two thousand miles to see you, only love does."

At Abbey's confused look, her mom explained that there was a SUV parked right behind hers with a Colorado license plate.

"I'm going to go now. He and you have a lot to talk about. I will not be a third wheel or a referee."

She left Abbey standing in the middle of the room. She walked into the kitchen to see Noland turning off the stove with a pan of cookies in his hand.

"Hi Noland, my name is Maggie. Don't go too easy on her but when you see those sparks in her eyes back down a little and let her think about it. I will be back tomorrow and I expect to see you." She kissed him on the cheek and left, thinking the whole while he would make a great son-in-law and father.

After Maggie left, Noland went outside and grabbed his bags. He was not leaving until they resolved everything and Abbey agreed to marry him. When he came back in he locked the door, turned off the lights and walked to the closed door he saw Maggie come out of. He didn't see Abbey sitting in the living room so he figured she was still in that room. He guessed Abbey forgot about him because she was in the bed. He just climbs in beside her.

"You know we have a lot to talk about."

"That's the second time you have repeated yourself to me. Can we talk later? I'm just too tired right now."

"Yes we can talk later. I took the cookies out of the stove and turned the stove off."

"Thank you."

"You're welcome. Is it okay if I hold you?"

"Yes it is okay and I was going to request that you hold me. I missed being held by you."

"I miss holding you."

?Thirty Six?

The shrill of the telephone woke them both up.

"Hello. Yes. I'm okay, I was just sleeping that's all. Sorry that I worried you. What can I do for you, Leland? Yes, he's right here. Do you want to talk to him?" She handed Noland the phone and made a move to get up. Noland pulled her down and closer to him so she would not go anywhere.

"Yes, I made it down here okay. I know I promised to call but I was tired. No, that is not the reason why. No, I haven't had a chance to ask her, yet. I will call you when I do and let you know the answer. Damn, Leland okay, hold on I'll do it now."

"Leland sounds like he was really worried about you."

"Not worried about me, just impatient and nosy."

"Impatient, I don't see how him wanting to know if you made it okay is being impatient?"

"He wants to know what your answer is to my question."

"You didn't ask me any questions."

"I really don't want to do this with my brother listening in but I really don't have a choice right now."

"Do you what?"

"Abbey, will you marry me?" Then he pulled a ring out of his pocket.

"Noland, I don't know what to say. We haven't resolved any of our issues."

"It's either yes you want to marry me or no you don't want to marry me."

"Of course, I want to marry you."

Picking up the phone, Noland said, "She said yes." then hung up the phone.

"Why did you hang up on Leland?"

"Abbey I love you and I could care less where we live as long as we live together every day for the rest of our lives. Leland does not need to be in on what we decide to do or where to live. It's our decision and I don't need or want any interference. Also, just so you know I was not going to accept no for an answer."

"I wouldn't have given you a no either. I do love you, Noland and that's the real reason why I left. I realized that I could not even keep my own promise to myself. I fell in love with the very first guy I saw. My very own incredible Snowman. I think your home will be the perfect place to raise a family."

"Then we should get married in Miami. I think a May wedding would be great. I could stay down here until then. I have Adrian watching over the shop and I talked to Lily."

"Stop talking Noland." Abbey said after she put her hand over his mouth. "Let's solve one problem at a time. May will not work, but this month will be better for the pregnant bride." She finished with a smile.

Noland snatched her hand off his mouth. "You're going to have a baby?"

"No, we are going to have a baby. Bringing in the New Year the way we did created a baby. I was getting prepared to come up there and insert myself back into your life. My mom dropped off things I would need to be up there during the rest of the winter months. I have already sublet my condo."

"What would you have done?"

"I would have used the house key that I still have on my keyring. Not a breaking and entering crime, since I have a key. I would beg for forgiveness at being afraid to believe in love at first sight. I would follow you wherever you went until you forgave me and put me out of my misery."

"So you would have been stalking me?"

"Call it what you want but I call it strong-minded. Especially after I saw my ex last week, he had me thinking what in the world did I see in him. I finally came up with the answer: he was safe. "

"How did you manage to see your ex?'

"He came over with a sob story that I was the best thing he ever had. I left him standing outside, after I told him he was the worst mistake I ever made. Making a mistake is good because you learn from it. You were a mistake but the best mistake that I ever made."

"How was I a mistake and what did you learn?"

"You were a mistake because I had a job to do and I got involved with you. I learned that I can be myself with you. I learned to let go and enjoy the ride."

"Enjoy the ride, what ride?"

"Okay, I'm going to confess to you but don't get the big head."

"My head is already big."

"Ha ha, I was always, as you already know, self-conscious about my size."

"I love your shape or size. I love your body, but you already know that."

"Yes, but people like Lily always made me more self-conscious."

"Plain old jealousy, she was angry that I never viewed her as anything other than a sister."

"With me being self-conscious, I was uptight about sex. I could not relax enough to enjoy it. With you, I see how much you appreciate my body and I get to relax. This in turn, allows me to be able to reach a climax while having sex with you. You are the first guy I had sex with where I was able to reach an orgasm with. That's what I was thinking about the first two times we had sex. I couldn't believe that I could achieve an orgasm. I was shocked I could not control my jabber. I expect no less from here on out."

"Is that going to be in our marriage contract?"

"You best believe it, right after I will love her for the rest of my life."

"Wow, you do have a high demand."

"You started something and you better keep it up. I am forever spoiled now. Do you think you will be able to handle my demands?"

"Yes, I will be able to handle anything that you demand of me, just as long as you tell me what's going on. You keeping Lily's remarks among yourself hurt me."

"I didn't want to see her get fired because of me. You have known her longer than me."

"True, I have known her longer, but I want you in my life. You also could have told me about why you were there and that my brother was not helping."

"Okay, I will trust you more with what's going on in my everyday life."

"That's all I ask." His father was right, his love did come at a cost. It cost him three months of agony, but in the end love worked it out.

?Thirty Seven?

The wedding happened that next Friday. Noland was not happy with the wait. They applied for the marriage license on Monday and then had to wait three days, since they did not take the twelve month marriage course. During those three days there were a lot of things that had to be done. Abbey wanted to get married in a formal gown, so he had to find a suit and a location that was romantic enough to him for them to get married at. If they were going to be formally dressed they were not getting married on the beach. Now having the beach in the background was doable. He decided on one of the Resort and Spa locations and it had an opening for Friday afternoon.

The wedding was simple and elegant. Only his parents and her parents were able to make it. It was a last minute wedding that caught a lot of media attention. He did not know that his brothers and he were considered such a good catch to get that type of media attention. After the wedding his parents flew back to SnowMass Village.

Noland drove back to Abbey's condo with a smile on his face. He was glad that Abbey wanted to get married in formal clothing; it made the wedding pictures look great. Upon arriving at her condo, the parking space that was assigned to her had a vehicle parked behind hers.

"Why is he here?"

"Why is who here, Abbey?"

"My ex, maybe I didn't spell it out enough for him when he was here earlier."

"Well come on, we both will tell him."

"No fighting. I will not be doctoring you if you start fighting."

"Are you trying to say I'm going to need doctoring on?"

"Yes, if you punch him anywhere I will have to get you an ice pack for your hand and hear you complain about how much your hand hurts."

"Okay, I promise no fighting."

"Thank you, now let's get out."

"Hi Abbey, how are you doing today?"

"She's doing really well, Toad."

"It's Todd. Abbey, have you thought about what we talked about the last time I was here?"

Abbey could tell Todd was trying to make Noland mad and she did not want to start her marriage off like this.

"Actually Todd, I have and I want to introduce you to my husband, the joy and love of my life and the father of my unborn child Noland Snow."

"Your husband and unborn child, what are you talking about?"

"Yes, Toad, her husband as in bride and groom or husband and wife, until death do us part, matching wedding rings does any of this sound familiar to you? Do I need to educate you on what an unborn child is?"

"The name is Todd and not toad. Plus I believe I was talking to Abbey."

"I like the name Toad better. It suits you."

"Look Todd, today is my wedding day and I am planning on enjoying the rest of my day with my husband. Last year you had the opportunity to marry me but you chose my business partner. I have forgiven and now I want to forget you. The only thing you have given me while we were together was a headache, heartache and sexual frustration. Now I have moved on to bigger, better and brighter things."

"I think that's a pleasant clue for you to leave. On the way out try not to hit my vehicle, thanks."

Noland proceeded to sweep Abbey up in his arms to carry her over the threshold. He promised her as soon as they got to SnowMass Village he would carry her over their permanent home's threshold also.

Don't miss out!

Visit the website below and you can sign up to receive emails whenever PRESCILLA ROSS-YOUNG publishes a new book. There's no charge and no obligation.

https://books2read.com/r/B-A-JPZR-RUDWB

BOOKS2READ

Connecting independent readers to independent writers.